朵拉
上台表演

童趣出版有限公司编译　　　人民邮电出版社出版

亲爱的小朋友，欢迎跟朵拉一起加入探险的旅程。在这里，你将学到丰富有趣的知识，参与活泼好玩的游戏，认识乐于助人的朋友，相信这将是一个快乐神奇之旅，保证让你收获多多。还等什么，快出发吧！

朵 拉 对 你 说

　　小朋友，我们的探险就要开始了，你一定又兴奋又激动吧。我还有一个小小的要求，探险结束时，我要问你几个小问题，再交给你几个小任务，你能做到吗？你这么棒，你一定能行的！我相信你！

1.你知道什么是海盗吗？他们的生活是什么样的？
　　让妈妈帮你找一找关于海盗的资料。
2.你坐过船吗？你还见过什么样的船？
3.舵是做什么用的？它很重要吗？
4.自己动手，设计一艘小船，给它起个漂亮的名字。

嗨，我是朵拉。你想参加海盗剧演出吗？你答应了？太好了！赶紧换上演出服吧！

Hello! I'm Dora. Do you want to be in our pirate play? Great! Let's go put on our costumes!

哎呀！好像是海盗来了。你看到海盗了吗？

海盗小猪把我们装演出服的箱子搬走了！他们以为里面是金银财宝呢。

如果我们不把这个箱子夺回来，就不能打扮成海盗了，要是不能打扮成海盗，就不能演海盗剧了。

Uh-oh. That sounds like pirates. Do you see pirates?

The Pirate Piggies are taking our costume chest! They think it's full of treasure.

If we don't get the costumes back, we can't dress up like pirates. And if we can't dress up like pirates, then we can't put on our pirate play.

我们一定能夺回演出服，只要知道怎么走就行了。我们不知道路线的时候该向谁求助呢？没错，是地图！

We can get our costumes back. We just have to know where to go. Who do we ask for help when we don't know where to go? The Map!

地图说，海盗小猪把金银箱藏到了金银岛上。我们必须经过七海，通过唱歌桥，才能到达金银岛。

Map says the Pirate Piggies took the treasure chest to Treasure Island. We have to sail across the Seven Seas and go under the Singing Bridge, and that's how we'll get to Treasure Island.

你看到七海了吗？没错，就是这片海！我们可以坐那条小船划过去！

Do you see the Seven Seas? Yeah, there they are! We can use that boat to sail across!

太棒了！现在我们该过七海了。一起来数数吧。一，二，三，四，五，六，七。

Great! Now it's time to sail the Seven Seas. Let's count the Seven Seas together. one, two, three, four, five, six, seven.

数得真不错!
现在该找唱歌桥了。它到底在哪儿呢?

Good counting!
Now we need to find the Singing
Bridge. Where is the bridge?

看，就在那儿。我们走吧！
Yeah, there it is. Let's go!

唱歌桥正在唱一支很难听的歌。
划呀划，划小船，
轻轻地顺流而下。
愉快地划，愉快地划，
人生不过是面条一碗！

The Singing Bridge sings silly songs.
Row, row, row your boat,
Gently down the stream,
Merrily, merrily,
merrily, merrily,
Life is but a bowl of spaghetti!

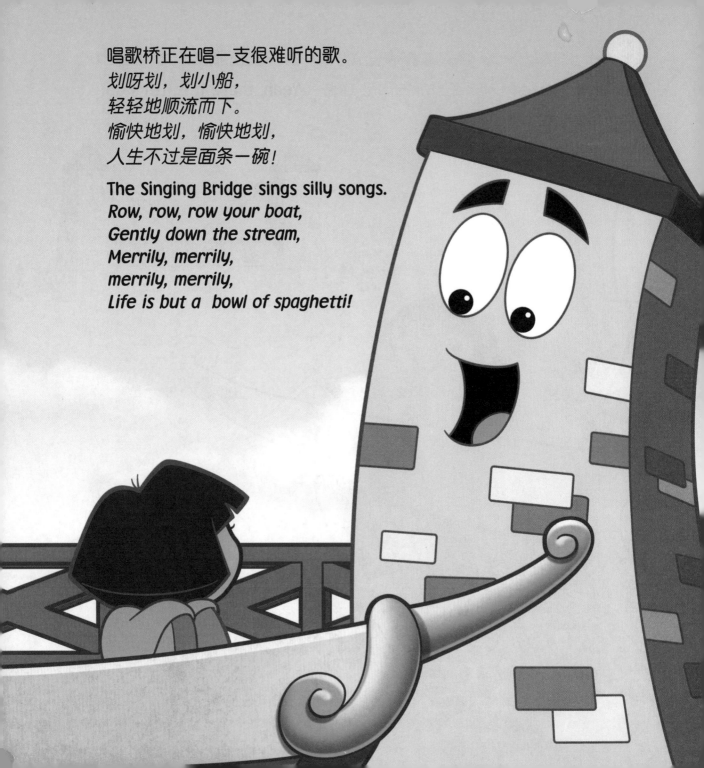

他唱错了，我们来教他正确的歌词，一起唱快乐的歌吧。

We have to teach him the right words. Let's sing the song the right way.

划呀划，划小船　　　轻轻地顺流而下。
愉快地划，愉快地划，　人生就是美好的梦！

Row, row, row your boat,
Gently down the stream,
Merrily, merrily, merrily, merrily,
Life is but a dream!

太好了，我们通过了唱歌桥！接下来要向金银岛出发了。你看到金银岛了吗？对，就在那儿！

Yay! We made it past the Singing Bridge! Next up is Treasure Island. Do you see Treasure Island? Yeah, there it is!

看，瀑布！埃沙必须赶紧调转舵轮，不然我们都会掉下去。

糟糕，舵轮坏了！也许书包里有东西能帮助我们。快，请大声说："书包！"

Look! There's a waterfall. Isa has to turn the wheel, or we'll go over the edge.

Uh-oh! The wheel broke! Maybe Backpack has something that will help us. Quick, say "Backpack!"

我们需要一样东西来固定舵轮。你看到胶带了吗？
对，就在那儿！太棒了！

We need something to fix the wheel. Do you see the sticky tape?

Yeah, there it is! Great!

埃沙，快转动舵轮！
唷嗬！我们终于绕开了瀑布。
快来！和我们一起去金银岛
夺回演出服吧！

Turn the wheel, Isa!
Whew! We made it past the waterfall.
Come on! Let's go to Treasure Island, and
get our costumes back!

我们终于来到了金银岛。现在一起去找金银箱吧。对了，我们可以用迪哥的望远镜。

We found Treasure Island. Now let's look for the treasure chest. We can use Diego's spotting scope.

金银箱在那里！快，伙伴们，让我们一起去夺回演出服！

There it is! Come on, mateys, let's go get our costumes back!

海盗小猪不想把装演出服的箱子还给我们。现在我们需要你的帮助。我数到三时，你就喊："把箱子还给我们！"准备好了吗？一，二，三，把箱子还给我们！

The Pirate Piggies say they won't give us back our treasure. We need your help. When I count to three, you need to say "Give us back our treasure!" Ready? One, two, three: Give us back our treasure!

真管用！太好了！海盗小猪说，你们可以把金银箱搬回去了！

It worked! Great! The Pirate Piggies say we can have our treasure chest back!

谢谢你帮我们夺回了演出服。这下我们可以表演
海盗剧了。开演吧！太好喽！

Thanks for helping us get our costumes back.
Now we can put on our pirate   play. We
did it! Hurray!

书包万岁！要是没有你和书包的帮忙，我们可就还不了书了！谢谢你！

Hooray for Backpack! We couldn't have done it without her or you! Thanks for helping!

门真的开了！现在我们总算可以按时还书了。
图书管理员瓦尔是不是从我的书包里拿了八本书出来呢？你能数清楚吗？

We did it! Now we can return my library books on time.
Can you count to make sure Val the librarian has all eight books from Backpack?

我们来到了图书馆。

真糟糕！门已经关了，不过我们可以用英语把门叫开。你只要说"open"，门就会打开。你会说"open"吗？

Here we are at the library.

Oh, no! The door is closed, but we can use English to open it. If you say, "open," the door will open. Can you say, "open"?

谢谢你帮我们赶跑了捣蛋鬼。现在我们可以划着小船过海龟河了。我们马上就到图书馆了，你看见图书馆了吗？

Thanks for helping us stop Swiper. Now we can cross Turtle River. We're almost at the library. Can you see it?

没错！救生衣！不好，我听到捣蛋鬼狐狸来了。他想偷我们的救生衣！你要是看见他就说："捣蛋鬼，不许偷东西！"

Right! Life jackets! Uh-oh. I hear Swiper the fox. He's trying to Swipe them! If you see him, say, "Swiper, no swiping!"

现在我们准备划着那只小船过海龟河。为了保证安全，我们在上船之前应该穿什么呢？看看书包里面吧！

Now we need to take that boat across Turtle River. Before we get into the boat what should we wear to be safe? Check Backpack!

对了，用绳子！我需要你帮忙一起把布茨拉出来。伸出你的双手，使劲地拉呀，拉呀，拉呀！你做得太好了！

Right, a rope! I need your help to pull Boots out. Use your hands and pull, pull, pull! Great job!

我们一起从书包里面找个东西帮帮布茨吧。你找到了吗?

Let's check Backpack for something to help Boots. Can you find it?

你找到了雨伞！真棒！

糟糕！那朵乌云带来的雨把地面全淋湿了，布茨陷进了黏乎乎的稀泥里。

You found the umbrella!

Oh, no! That storm cloud made the ground all wet. Now Boots is stuck in the Icky-Sticky Sand.

网剪破了，我们顺利通过了小矮人桥。接下来我们该去海龟河了，可是空中飘来一朵乌云，看来要下雨了！

We did it! We made it over the Troll Bridge. So next comes Turtle River, but there's a storm cloud! It's going to rain!

剪刀！没错。你能从我的书包里找到剪刀吗？我们要用这把剪刀把网剪破。

Scissors! That's right. Can you find a pair of scissors in my Backpack? We need them to cut through the net.

　　"这可是我最难的一个谜语哦，"小矮人神气地说，"用什么东西可以把这张网弄破？"
　　你知道答案吗？

　　"Here is one of my hardest quizzers," says the Grumpy Old Troll. "To cut through the net, use a pair of . . ."
　　What do you think the answer is?

我们来到小矮人桥下，可是小矮人要我们猜出他的谜语才能过桥。你能帮我们一起来猜这个谜语吗？

We made it to the Troll Bridge, but the Grumpy Old Troll won't let us cross unless we solve his riddle. Can you help us solve it?

地图说，我们得先过小矮人桥，然后过海龟河，就可以到图书馆了。

The map says we have to go over the Troll Bridge and then cross Turtle River. That's how we'll get to the Library.

现在我们得找一条能最快到达图书馆的路。当我们不知道路线的时候，应该问谁呢？没错，就是地图！它就在我的书包里。请一起说："地图！"

Now we have to find the quickest way to the library. Who do we ask for help when we don't know which way to go? The Map! There's a map inside my Backpack. Say, "Map!"

你好！我是朵拉，这是我的朋友书包！我要去图书馆还八本书，书包时刻准备着帮助我呢。我们一定得在图书馆关门之前赶到，你能帮我们吗？

你答应了？太好了！我们先要找到猴子布茨。你看见他了吗？

Hello! I'm Dora, and this is my friend Backpack! I need to return eight books to the library, and Backpack's going to help me. We have to get there before it closes. Will you help us too?

Great! First we need to find Boots the monkey. Do you see him?

亲爱的小朋友，欢迎跟朵拉一起加入探险的旅程。在这里，你将学到丰富有趣的知识，参与活泼好玩的游戏，认识乐于助人的朋友，相信这将是一个快乐神奇之旅，保证让你收获多多。还等什么，快出发吧！

朵 拉 对 你 说

　　小朋友，我们的探险就要开始了，你一定又兴奋又激动吧。我还有一个小小的要求，探险结束时，我要问你几个小问题，再交给你几个小任务，你能做到吗？你这么棒，你一定能行的！我相信你！

1. 为什么乌云能带来雨？你知道雨是怎么形成的吗？
2. 你去过图书馆吗？你知道在图书馆借书有什么程序和要求吗？
3. 我去图书馆都经过了哪些地方？你能试着画一张路线图吗？

朵拉的书包

童趣出版有限公司编译　　人民邮电出版社出版